TRICKIN' IS A TREAT

BRIANN DANAE

Trickin' Is A Treat

Cover designed by Beyond The Book Designs

Aleesa

"This is why I don't like dating broke men," I huffed in annoyance and locked my phone.

This was Coop's second time this month, making excuses as to why he couldn't take me out. Honestly, I can't even call it an excuse this time because I was over those. A grown man that can't afford to do anything was a complete turnoff. No, he didn't have to spend an absurd amount of money on me but sitting at home on his worn-down leather couch eating ramen noodles while he fucked off on the game was not ideal. Nothing wrong with ramen noodles at all, but I'm an adventurer. Take me out to places for an experience and a good time.

"Let me guess, that's Coop?" My cousin Kharisma questioned.

"Yes. I asked if he wanted to go to the haunted house, and he had the nerve to lie and say he'd already been."

"How'd you know he was lying?"

I sucked my teeth. "Because. The one I asked about is shut down. It hasn't reopened since that girl's family sued them and won last year."

Pits of Hell used to be a very popular haunted house in our city. Last year when a young girl died while she was leaving out, the owner's shut it down. According to the news and documents I read, the girl and her friends had completed the trail when an actor with a chainsaw came out of nowhere. He chased after the young girl, ended up tripping on a nearby cord, and the chainsaw sawed her face in half. That has been the most horrifying death I think I've ever heard of in all my life, on some *Final Destination* shit.

"That was a really horrible way to die," Kharisma shivered just thinking about it.

"I know, and Coop just lied for no reason. This isn't the first time, though. I seem to always catch him up, but that's okay. I'm going to find a man who doesn't mind spending money on me."

"Or, let him find you," she offered as we walked into *Ace Liquors*.

"Or that," I replied with a shrug.

It was the evening of Halloween, and we were still trying to decide what events we planned to attend. Before anything though, we had to pregame. While some people didn't participate in what many considered a holiday, I certainly did. Not just for the candy, parties, or alcohol, but the overall eeriness the season brought. Plus, I could let go of my inhibitions that's been holding me back for the majority of the year and become a different person. Thankfully, I'd purchased my costume well before all of the good ones had been picked over in my size.

"Dark or clear tonight?" I asked, moseying down the aisle.

"I'm okay with whatever you choose. Don't forget, I have some edibles from the girl who works with you."

I did an about-face and frowned. "Who?"

"Simmy."

"Oh, hell. Her weird ass. We're going to be high as Cooter Brown."

It was Kharisma's turn to frown in confusion. "Who is that?"

Chuckling, I shook my head. It was an old metaphor that I didn't feel like getting into.

"No one. Let's go with Tequila. We can never go wrong with that."

"I meeean, you can but who really cares?" Kharisma giggled.

Walking out of the aisle after grabbing a bottle of white Tequila by a local brand that we've had before, we were stopped by a woman posted up at a table in the back of the store.

"Hey, ladies! Come on over here and take a free shot."

I was all for free alcohol, and inside of a liquor store? Why not. Scattered about the table were plastic throw away shot cups and a variation of bottles of liquor I hadn't had before. Glancing at the woman's nametag that read, Jennifer, I gave her a smile.

"What all do you have?"

"Just about anything, but for you… here's something special."

I hope she isn't trying to poison me, I thought while she poured some type of sky-blue liquid into a cup.

"Don't worry; I'm not poisoning you," she said with ease.

My eyes bucked, thinking I'd said that aloud but I know I hadn't. "Huh?" I questioned, just to make sure.

"You look a bit apprehensive. Trust me; it's smooth."

"Well, I don't want smooth," Kharisma let her know. "Give me the strongest liquor you have."

"Coming right up, darling."

Once she poured Kharisma's, she gave us a smile.

"Alright. Be sure to make a wish while taking your shot."

"Ooh, like blowing out your birthday cake candles and making a wish," Kharisma beamed, ready as ever to oblige.

"And what does this wish grant?" I asked.

"Whatever you want it to, I suppose. That's between you and the wish-granting authorities. Drink up!"

For some reason, I was hesitant about taking this shot, but before I could prove Jennifer's suspicions right, Kharisma and I touched cups, tapped the table, and tossed our shots back. Of course, I made my wish like requested – two actually – and grinned. Hopefully, with the full moon tonight, my wish would be granted immediately. It was smooth she said. And a bit sweet. I wasn't expecting that. It wasn't as strong as I anticipated but had just enough kick to it.

"Good, right?" Jennifer asked.

"Very good, actually. Do you guys sell that in store?"

Jennifer shook her head no. "Nope. Not yet. Keep this between us."

Pulling a few dollars from my purse, I handed them to her. "Will do."

After paying for our bottle, Kharisma and I were headed out of the store when a guy named Wayne, we went to college with walked in the store with a few of his friends. Fine ass friends, might I add. All different assortments of chocolate, height, weight, and build.

"Ladies, ladies," Wayne grinned, giving us both hugs. "I see y'all getting ready to turn up tonight."

"Of course. We don't have any plans as of yet though," Kharisma told him.

"It is a lot going on tonight, but y'all might as well slide to our Halloween party."

"We didn't know anything about it," I told him.

"Yeah, it was sort of last minute, but you know how we do. It's invite-only, so I'll text you the address."

He was talking to Kharisma when he mentioned texting. Wayne was cute, but he was a hoe. Me and male whores never worked out. Soon as I caught wind of some hoe shit they were on, so was I, and our phase was over.

"Okay," Kharisma said, and we walked out of the store.

In the car, I buckled my passenger seatbelt and rubbed the back of my neck. That shot wasn't all that big, but it had me hot already.

"You okay?" Kharisma asked, pulling out of the lot.

"Yeah. A little hot. You still mess around with Wayne?"

She grinned, which meant yes. "Mhm. Sometimes. He's fun to be around and has good dick," she shrugged. "Why not?"

"So, if you see a girl all over him tonight at their party, then what?"

"Then that's on him. I promise not to ruin our night by starting a fight."

"With anyone," I added. She was known to start fights with Wayne, but I didn't need her trying to fight any women over him either.

"With anyone. Plus, I'll look too cute, and my skirt is much too short."

While she opted on being a substitute teacher, I went for a sexy cat woman outfit. It wasn't the regular long sleeve leather suit either. Mine was a leather onesie with a deep v-cut that exposed my cleavage, black fishnet stockings, a garter belt, a black cat ear mask, and thigh-high leather boots. I'd already tried it on and sent pictures to my mom, who had encouraged me to be a bit more daring. She was all for the sexy costumes, seeing as though that's how she met my dad back in the day.

I'll never forget her telling me how she was a cowgirl, and my stepdad just so happened to be the horse. I still gag to this day when she tries to tell us why we should dress up on Halloween. Her theory was, we'd find a man like she did. I'd been going to Halloween parties since high school, so maybe this year would be my lucky year.

Aleesa

M akeup? *Check.*
Wristlet? *Check.*

Sexy, leave nothing to the imagination? *Check.*

Drunk? *Double check.*

Between the shot that was doing something highly eerie to my body, the Tequila we made into mixed drinks, and the bite-size fruity pebble edible I'd taken, I was floating. The temperature had dropped just a bit, but not too drastically. Plus, we didn't dress for the weather; we dressed for the occasion. We learned that lesson early on in college.

"Why do I feel like I've been in this neighborhood before?" I questioned, gazing out the passenger window as we drove by immaculate homes.

"You probably have."

As Kharisma drove to our destination for the night, the familiarity of having been here before hit me. I never really had déjà vu, but my mind had made up that we'd been here before. As if squinting my eyes would assist me with going down memory lane, they formed into slits as we pulled into a circular driveway at the end of the block. The driveway easily held over thirty vehicles, and a home – more like a mansion – that I'm sure held triple that in people.

"Who the hell lives here?" I squeaked, taking in the well-lit landscape.

"I'm not sure. I think this house used to be on foreclosure until one of Wayne's friends bought it."

"His friend who?"

Kharisma shrugged. "I can't think of his name right now. I'm sure he'll be inside though."

I was hoping he was as well. If a man our age had purchased this home, I wanted to meet him. You know... for research purposes. Whoever this nigga was, he was living large. Decorated perfectly for the occasion, jack-o-lanterns, skeletons, floating ghosts, spider webs with fake spiders to match, and much more set the mood. What tied it all together was the thick layer of fog floating atop the manicured lawn.

Pulling down the visor, I checked to make sure my black lipstick still coated my full lips. Kharisma handed me a piece of gum to pop in my mouth as I fluffed my fresh braid-out that hung past my shoulders.

"If you didn't have on those cat ears, I'd think you were a dominatrix," Kharisma mused, giving me a side-eye.

I chuckled. "I'm more of a submissive, but who's to say the roles can't be reversed?"

"Oh, goodness. Let us get out of this car."

Following suit, I adjusted my boobs and stepped out of the car. A few partygoers were hanging around outside when we walked up. The catcalls – figuratively, thanks to my outfit – started before we could make it completely up what seemed like hundreds of stairs. A bit thicker than me, Kharisma's ass cheeks were playing peek-a-boo in her plaid skirt, while the white button-up shirt was tied under her boobs, showing off her nonexistent waist. My leather ensemble felt painted on and actually fit a bit snugger than it had some weeks ago, but I wasn't complaining one bit.

At the door, we were greeted by a giant man, dressed as Frankenstein. I loved how everyone was in costume.

"Evening, ladies. Please pick a treat from the pumpkin."

Holding out the pumpkin-shaped basket, Kharisma giddily dug her hand inside. Retracting it, she frowned seeing a pack of candy corn.

"Eww. Who the hell eats candy corn? Can I go again?"

He shook his head. "No can do. One treat for now. Your turn."

Slowly, I eased my hand inside, swooshed the candy around, and pulled out a plastic egg.

"An egg?" I questioned, and Frankenstein simply shrugged. "It's not Easter. This better not be empty."

Popping it open, my eyes damn near fell from their sockets.

"What the hell!" Kharisma squealed. "Money!?"

And money it was—three-hundred dollars to be exact. As confused as I was by not receiving candy, there was no way I was trading this in for some.

"Wow," I mumbled lowly while staring at the three crisp hundred-dollar bills.

"Ladies, we have other guests trying to get in," he let us know.

Moving out of the pathway of the door, we stepped off to the side where an empty dining room was. Placing the money in my wristlet, we followed the upbeat tunes of some hip-hip Halloween music.

TRICKIN' IS A TREAT

The strobe lights and dancing bodies only seemed to intensify my jovial mood.

"Have you had enough to drink?" Kharisma semi-shouted over the loud music.

I nodded as my eyes blinked in a slower than usual manner. Making our way through the crowd to where Wayne and his crew were, I dismissed a few men trying to gain my attention. As soon as Wayne's eyes landed on Kharisma, they warmed and his grin widened. Quick strides had him in our face within seconds.

"Shiiit," he exaggerated, making Kharisma blush while I smiled. "You gon' write me up for misbehaving Miss. Substitute Teacher?"

"It's Mrs. Donovan to you."

Wayne's head tilted back some. "Oh, word? You a freak and cheating on yo' nigga?"

Kharisma slapped his arm. "Shut up, silly."

"I'm saying. I don't mind making up for what that nigga can't do. I need a few tutoring sessions after class anyway. Show me how much further this skirt can go up and what's underneath it."

Without thought, he gripped Kharisma's bare ass while pulling her into him. I'd never seen Wayne behave this way, especially with my cousin, and I didn't want to start. Clearing my throat, Wayne glanced my way and gave me his boyish grin that I'm sure was the sole reason Kharisma had given him the pussy in the first place.

"Aleesa. Girl, you thicker than cold grits."

"You have issues, Wayne. This party turned out bigger than I expected. While you were talking about some last-minute plans."

He glanced around and shrugged. "Word of mouth travels fast. Especially when we do something. Y'all just got here?"

"Yeah. About ten minutes ago. Thanks for the door prize."

"You can take all that damn candy home when this is over. Nobody gonna eat that shit."

"My nieces and nephew will."

My attention altered from Wayne to the sultry, resonant baritone that summoned me to look his way. He spoke in almost a whisper but was loud and clear in my head. It had literally invaded every part of my brain in seconds. I hadn't gotten his name yet, but I didn't give a fuck what it was. I wanted him.

Dressed in the ultimate Hugh Hefner attire only much better, he wore a burgundy robe that showcased ripples of chocolate abs and defined pecs. The gold Cuban link chain around his neck contrasted deliciously against his skin tone. A healthy, well-groomed beard framed juicy lips. The black silk pajama pants left nothing to my imagination as it seemed his dick was begging for me to stroke it. He was *heavy*! Unsure if my eyes were growing bigger or his dick was expanding, I quickly diverted my stare before I gave everyone in this party a tutorial on how to give the perfect blow job.

When we locked eyes, his facial expression was neutral as if I hadn't just eye-fucked him. I most definitely needed another drink now. Instead of the pipe I'm sure came along with his costume, he was puffing on a blunt that smelled divine and exotic. Thick smoke seeped from his plush lips before he licked them, causing my nipples to go rock hard.

What the hell is happening right now?

How was I this turned on and didn't even know this man's name? It has to be the liquor.

"Are you enjoying yourself?" he asked, and I simply nodded my head.

My tongue was heavy, forcing me to be unable to use my words. With a dry mouth, I swallowed hard and broke my gaze when Kharisma shook my shoulder.

"Leesa, are you alright?" she questioned with worry etched on her face.

"Yeah, yeah. I'm good. Why?"

"You were literally just staring off into space like someone was talking to you."

Hurriedly, I glanced around for a sign of the man I'd just been salivating over. I shouldn't have had to search far, seeing as though he was just in front of me, but he was nowhere to be found. *Where did he go?* My mind was definitely playing tricks on me, or was he a magician?

"T-There wasn't a guy in a robe that just walked up to us?"

Wayne looked at Kharisma and shook his head while chuckling. "Whatever drugs y'all on, keep 'em to y'all self. Shorty trippin'."

Ignoring Wayne, I lowkey continued to look around for the fine man who fucked up my head that quickly. Coming up short, I chucked it up as me having been daydreaming.

"Let's go get us a drink," Kharisma suggested.

Stepping into the kitchen that was big enough to be an apartment, we waited in line to grab a drink. While I snagged another mixed drink from the bartender, Kharisma grabbed a bottle of water. I was hotter than I should've been and not because of my leather outfit. After a few sips of my drink, I handed it to Kharisma so that we could swap. No way was I about to be super drunk.

TRICKIN' IS A TREAT

Making our way back toward the dancefloor, the DJ was still killing it with the Halloween jams. Kharisma and I hit the robot to *A Nightmare on My Street* and busted out laughing when I did the run it man in slow motion. When *Disturbia* by Rihanna came on, I couldn't help but dance like I was back in college at one of the white clubs. Hands in the air and eyes closed, I snapped my fingers and let the song take over my body.

This was the type of fun I missed having. Too bad I didn't have a man to appreciate my dance moves and sexy outfit. Coop had definitely missed out, but I was hoping for him to be far removed from my mind before tonight ended.

Be careful what you wish for.

My eyes peeled open, and heart rate slowed. In search of the familiar voice I'd heard from earlier, I looked around as everyone seemed to move in slow motion. Even the music had crept to a downtempo. As I reached for Kharisma, the task took forever. When she was finally in my grasp, her lips moved in a languid manner. Shaking my head, my fuzzy mind blurred as my eyes closed. When they opened, *he* was standing in front of me again.

"Are you following me?" I asked just above a whisper, and he grinned.

This time, I got a glimpse of two gold fangs and a set of pearly white teeth that made him even sexier.

"Yo, Aleesa. This my bro Rich. This his crib and shit," Wayne introduced him.

Rich. I wonder what his full name is.

It perfectly describes every aspect of him from what I could tell.

Rich skin.

Rich pockets.

Rich nigga dick.

There was absolutely no way he looked like *this* and had broke dick. Well, I take that back. He could've. That broke dick be good sometimes and comes from a medium-ugly nigga. I would know. It sold me all these promises and made me believe them. Coop had broke nigga dick for sure.

"We've met before," I let him know.

"For real? That's what's up. I don't know how; this nigga is a loner."

"Fuck you," Rich chuckled, then focused on me. "Where did we meet, gorgeous?"

In my dreams, is what I wanted to say. "Um. I can't quite remember, but nice seeing you again. You have an amazing home."

"'Preciate that. Don't get lost and give yourself a tour. It might take a while for us to find you."

"It's that big?"

He licked his lips, clearly amused by my choice of words. I meant his home, not his dick, even though I'd already peeped and confirmed that *it* indeed was.

"Find out for yourself."

Before I could get trapped in his honey eyed gaze, I broke our stare down. When he and Wayne walked away, I admired his strong back and shoulders from behind. He even walked like *it* was heavy. A chill inched down my spine.

"Why have you never introduced me to him?" I asked Kharisma.

"I literally forgot. He's never around that much. I'm surprised he even went along with having a party here."

I couldn't blame him. The place was laid. I'm sure a couple of people have already done some snooping around. After a few more songs were danced to, the DJ announced that it was time for them to vote for the best costume. While there were plenty of well-dressed people, only a few had gone all out.

A dark skin beauty dressed up as Storm won out of the women, and a midget man dressed up as Michael Myers – affectionately known now as Mekyale Myurs thanks to Twitter – won. Honestly, he deserved to the way he had the crowd laughing. He was rocking a fucked up dry wig with split ends, a dingy navy jumpsuit, a deflated mask that was too big for his head and carried a knife just like Michael. What made his costume even funnier was him stomping around the party like he was looking for his next victim.

As the party began to wind down, I realized using the bathroom in this outfit wasn't going to be simple at all and was pissed about it. Bouncing from foot to foot, I tried finding Rich to ask where the nearest bathroom was. Of course, he was nowhere to be found.

"I'm gonna go find the ladies' room," I let Kharisma know.

"I'll come with you. My bladder is about to burst."

"Ask Wayne where the closest one is."

She waved me off. "Girl, no. We'll find one. It can't be that hard."

She was wrong. It took a full two minutes for us to locate a bathroom that was down a long, elegantly decorated hall. Crisp white walls with high-end pictures decorated them, while large floor sculptures were placed perfectly. The further we ventured from the crowd and noise from the party, the calmer I felt. Our heels clicked in a soothing rhythm against the marble flooring. My mind was still stuck on how Rich could afford such property and why he wanted to live here of all places. Granted, it was quiet but much too spacious for my liking.

"You can go first since I have too much clothing to maneuver," I told her once we reached our destination.

"Okay. I'll be quick."

Pulling my phone from my clutch, I saw I had a bunch of notifications. The one that stood out the most was a CashApp payment from my ex-boyfriend Kent. I was confused as to why he would send me one hundred dollars randomly when we hadn't talked in months. Knowing him, it was probably his way of trying to get my attention. I was always grateful for free money, but he wasn't about to hear from me. Replying to the payment with a heart emoji was all the response I was giving.

"Who you texting?" Kharisma asked, walking out of the bathroom.

"Kent sent me a hundred dollars on CashApp. Isn't that weird?"

"Hell no. Money is money. You must have some type of magical touch on you tonight. First the egg, now this. Let me rub your head for good luck," she joked, making us laugh.

"Girl, bye. I'll buy you some food when we leave."

"Even better. Ya' girl could smash some chicken right now."

Leaving her in the hall after she unzipped me, I stepped inside the bathroom and rushed in a delicate manner to remove my onesie and garter belt. Sliding my stockings down, I squatted over the toilet seat and sighed as I relieved myself.

At the sink, I pumped the pumpkin spice scented foam soap into my hands and turned the water on. Glancing up to check my appearance in the mirror, I gasped loud and flinched hard when I saw Rich standing behind me. Hastily, I turned on my heels, and sure enough there he was. He invaded my personal space as my chest began to tighten. I was immobile under his intense, lustful eyes. The only thing moving was my eyeballs. They scattered to the door then back to him, trying to recollect when and how he'd gotten in here. I'd pinch myself to see if this was real, but the smell of his cologne shifting the scent infiltrating my nostrils was enough proof that this was.

He didn't speak. Rich simply pressed his hard body against mine. His dick stretched down the side of my thigh as it rested in his pants, and I so badly wanted to reach out and touch it.

Touch it.

My eyes bucked. Could he read my mind? He *could* read my fucking mind. While I should've been scared, the tight grip around my neck and sensual kiss along my clavicle and shoulder made me follow his command. Girth *and* length were hard to come by, but Rich did not disappoint in either department. Firm strokes from my hand had him groaning against my ear.

"You deserve to be spoiled and put up somewhere," he let be known.

I smirked. "Oh, really?"

"Yeah."

"I'm not a put-up type of woman."

"Not put away from the world, Aleesa. Shown off to it."

The rapid knocks on the door broke my... *what the fuck was that*? Feeling detached from reality only to be pulled back had my mind gone. Touching my neck where Rich's lips had or hadn't been, my body trembled. The only person in this bathroom was me, but his presence was heavily felt.

"Aleesa! You okay in there?"

"Y-Yeah," I muttered, washing my hands for real

this time. "I'm okay. Just keep getting mind-fucked thanks to whatever drugs I seem to be on."

Keeping what happened inside the bathroom to myself, we made our way back to the party. Most of the people had begun to leave. The DJ was playing music that let everyone know that they didn't have to go home, but sure as hell couldn't stay here. With the lights now on, I was granted a good look at some of the partygoers. In true party fashion, some were drunk as hell, including Mr. Mekyale himself, who wobbled up to my knee.

Looking down, I held back my laugh. "Hello," I spoke.

"What's up. Some of us are going bar crawling if you want to go."

"No, thanks. I've had enough to drink."

He shrugged. "Suit yourself. Have a good night."

"You too."

Once almost everyone was gone, Wayne gathered the remainder of people in the kitchen. There were a few of his boys, four of them, while three women stayed behind as well. Like I should've known she'd be doing, Kharisma was drunkenly munching on some chicken and grinning while Wayne whispered something in her ear. She nodded and he clapped his hands together. Lord only knows what she just agreed to.

"A'ight so look," Wayne started. "Y'all trying to play a game?"

"Yeah."

"I'm down."

"Hell yeah."

"Does it involve money?"

"Yessir!"

The round of affirmative responses let me know they'd possibly played this game before. So, I was the bullheaded one and disagreed.

"I don't usually like playing games."

"You'll love this one."

That was Rich.

We locked eyes, and he smirked. That same intense gaze settled in his eyes. Welp. If he said I'd love it, then that's what it'd be. Hopefully, whatever game it was didn't get me into any more trouble than I already was.

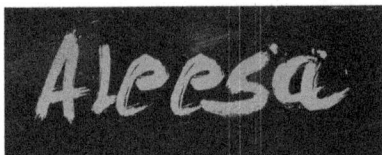

3

Aleesa

This was *not* the type of game I was prepared for.

I'm not sure along the course of the past couple of hours when my edible decided to smack the fuck out of me, but this high was *too* intense. Taking deep breaths, I looked around the circle of people to see had anyone noticed my spike of anxiety. A few seats away from me, Rich peeped what was going on and came to sit by me.

Soothingly, he rubbed my back and whispered in my ear, "Breathe. Slowly. Don't let it take over you. Here," he handed me a bottle of something that had me giving him a skeptical look. "Sip some of this."

"What is this?"

"Something that'll make you feel."

"Feel what?"

"Whatever you want."

Right now, the only thing on my mind was coming down. So, while sipping whatever this was, I asked for it to make me feel less in the clouds but still buzzed enough to enjoy the night. After a few minutes, my heart rate was normal, and I didn't feel like I was about to have a panic attack. Peering up at Rich, I gave him a smile.

"Thank you for that. How'd you know?"

"I'm just in tune with you."

"You don't know me."

"I know enough. You're up next."

He tilted his head in Wayne's direction, who was asking me a question. Somehow, we ended up playing this erotic card game of *Would You Rather*. But it was the Halloween edition.

"Okay. What're my choices?"

"Would you rather have sex in the middle of a hayride field or in a cemetery?"

"Easy. A hayride field. I'd never disrespect the dead like that."

Kharisma chuckled. "You wouldn't be scared of people catching you?"

"No. I actually like that thought of that."

"Me too! I thought I was the only one," the woman dressed up as Storm yelled out.

I shrugged like it was nothing because it really wasn't. "Nope. Just a simple fantasy."

"You on that, huh?" Wayne chuckled and lifted his eyebrows at Rich.

Rich flipped him off, making me laugh.

"Okay, okay. Rich, you're next," Kharisma told him. "This is a boring one, but still goes along with the theme and needs answers because I'm curious. Would you rather trick on a woman before you got the pussy, or have her give it up as a treat first?"

"I don't mind trickin' at all."

"Okaaaay!" Kharisma dragged as she and the other girls gave high-fives. "I heard that. What you say, Rich? It ain't tricking if you got it."

"And baby, he has it all," some girl said.

I didn't mean to, but I cut my eyes in her direction. Yes, I was very much so being territorial over Rich. I knew he was fair game right now, but not for long. He was talking my language. Adjusting my legs, I faced him.

"So, you're admitting to being a trick?"

"If that's what you consider buying a woman nice things she wants and providing for her, then I guess so."

"And this is without ever sampling the pussy?"

"She gon' give that up regardless and not because I spent some money on her. Women already know if they're sleeping with a man or not on the first date. We might as well blow a few bands before I fuck her good and have her in her feelings and have to spend more money anyway."

Whew. "Well, alrighty then. I guess this game is over."

The women cracked up laughing at me, but I was serious. I knew from the minute I saw him that I wanted to fuck. It was that simple. But I was going to play these games first. If it happened, it happened.

"Nah. I'ma have to disagree, bro," another guy named Bryan vocalized, shaking his head.

"Aye," Rich tossed his hands in the air. "This *rich* nigga lifestyle ain't for the weak."

"This nigga," Wayne cracked as we all laughed.

"Well, Rich. Women do like being spoiled every now and then, so thank you," Kharisma let him know. "You niggas be quick to ask for some pussy straight from the mouth that told us no."

"Man, nah. Y'all will meet a nigga and on the first day expect for him to pay yo' rent, get yo' nails done and shit. Like damn, baby. Can I get to know you first?"

"No!" All the women yelled.

"Y'all on bullshit," Wayne laughed.

"That's y'all! I honestly don't feel like it's an insult to ask a nigga I'm dating for money," I let them all know.

"Why not? You don't know that man's financial status. He could be down to his last," Bryan tried to explain.

"And I could be down to my last bit of groceries and ass. You think he ain't gone still ask for some?"

He laughed and nodded his head at that. "A'ight. You right, but damn."

"Nope. Unt, unt. The same way I can provide for you when you ask for something is the same way you should be able to provide for me, even though I can get it on my own. I don't see the issue at all."

"Me either. Men all have different mindsets," Rich said.

"Hell yeah, cause I'm sticking to what the fuck I said," Wayne laughed.

"And watch you not get any pussy tonight," Storm laughed.

Looking over at Kharisma, he nicked her chin with his index finger and grinned. "Shitting me."

"Boy, whatever," Kharisma laughed. "Anyway. Back to the game."

"Let's take some more shots first," one of Storm's friends said.

I was already feeling mellowed out, so I was going to pass on the drinks. While everyone poured up shots in the kitchen, Rich reached for my hand to help me up from the couch.

"Walk with me somewhere. I want to show you something."

"As big as this house is, we gon' be walking forever."

Without a struggle, he picked me up, and I wrapped my arms around his neck.

"You done complaining?"

I nodded with a smirk. "Yes."

On the walk to wherever he was taking me, I couldn't help but snuggle into the crook of his neck. His masculine scent, warm skin, and strong hold around me made me feel safer than I'd ever felt. The cool breeze along my skin made me peel my eyes open to see where he had brought us.

The view from the balcony was one I'd only seen on HGTV. As if this house needed any more space, the balcony wrapped around, having a grill and sitting area along with it. There were large windows that seemed to stretch into the night sky you couldn't see inside of. Now on my feet, I faced him.

"Please tell me why you need all of this house and it's just you."

"I like my space."

I crossed my arms over my chest. "Seriously? That's all?"

"Yeah. What other answer were you looking for?"

"I don't know, but surely not just because you like space."

"And because I can afford it."

I chuckled. "Obviously. This is an amazing view."

"Tell me about it."

I caught his gaze, but it wasn't on the view I was taking in. It was on me. Walking up behind me as I stood at the railing, Rich wrapped one arm low around my waist. Situating himself behind me with his erection boldly letting me know it was also present, I relaxed in his arms.

The full moon was settled high in the sky and bright as ever. Knowing I should've been at home doing my full moon ritual, I semi-chastised myself. Before I could get too deep in my thoughts, Rich's lips once again and for real this time, caressed my neck so softly. A moan escaped me as I realized I was willing to do whatever for and to him.

"What were you on tonight?" he asked, with his beard tickling my ear.

My mind jumbled for a bit trying to gauge what his question meant.

"The drugs."

"Oh," I cleared my throat. "An edible, but that's it."

"You sure?"

"Yes. Do you know something I don't? I felt like you could read my mind and kept appearing though you weren't really there."

"That was all your doing. I'm just here to grant your wishes."

As he massaged my breasts through my costume, I thought back to earlier in the evening before our night got started. Everything was normal until I took whatever it was Jennifer gave me at the liquor store. All I did was make a wish or two while taking my shot. Who would've known they'd actually come true hours later?

"You know what I asked for?"

"Tell me," he commanded while slowly pulling my costume down, making it pool at my feet. When he had unzipped it, I had no clue. My head was too far gone.

Every touch from him had me releasing a moan, and he had hardly done anything yet. With a firm smack to my ass, my back arched, and ass poked harder into him.

"Don't make me tell you twice."

"For you to fuck me."

"Where?"

"Right here, where everyone can see us."

Getting caught was just one of my fantasies. Having people watch me have sex was another. Thankfully, Rich and his immaculate ass home had just the type of windows to not only explore my sexual fantasy but act it out as well. I couldn't see inside the window once he had my ass up against it, but I knew his house guests could.

All inhibitions aside, because there was no room for pride when it was time to fuck, I tugged his silk pants down and freed his erection. While he fetched a condom from his pants pocket, I stroked his length after coating it with the wetness from between my legs. It'd been present all night, waiting for him to put it to good use.

And Rich did exactly that.

With both legs in the crooks of his arms, Rich slid into me slowly, feeding me every last inch of his dick. There was so much I had to tell myself to breathe while my head fell back.

"Uuuuh! Your dick is so big," I whimpered as he

pulled out and pushed back in me. "I don't think I can take it."

"You can do whatever the fuck you want. Be a big girl, Aleesa."

I was trying to be a big girl, but that dick was bigger. It stretched me out so deliciously good and had my eyes rolling to the top of my head. Holding on tight, Rich bounced me on his pole as if he fucked for sport. With ease, my slick walls accepting all of him while our skin clapped loudly and echoed into the night air.

"Fuck!" he spat, holding me still. "This shit too wet. Uggh. Don't do that."

Contracting my pussy muscles around him, I smiled as I rotated my hips and fucked him back. He wanted me to be a big girl, so that's what he was going to get. Slamming my back against the window, I screamed loud as he dug deeper, hitting my g-spot. Kissing my lips, he stuck his tongue in my mouth and kissed me with an urgency I'd never experienced before.

"Ohmygooosh!" My words slurred, mind turned to complete mush, and mouth dropped wide open.

In and out, up and down, Rich delivered the type of ssexual pleasure I had wished for. The type that I could willingly have with a man who knew what I wanted. My hold on him tightened as my legs quaked with an impending orgasm. When he sucked one of my nipples into his mouth, I lost it.

"That's it," he groaned in my ear. "You know what to do. Mmm, fuck yeah. Good girl."

He praised me for my obedient pussy cumming on his command. Rich wasn't too far behind. When I felt his legs buckle a bit, I urged him to let me down. I'd been daydreaming about sucking his dick all night.

Dropping into a squat, he snatched the condom off as I greedily took him into my mouth. Spit dripped down my chest as I swirled my tongue around his pole. When he forced my head back to stay planted against the window, I knew for sure I had met my match. With his hands planted firmly on the window above my head, I let him fuck my mouth until he was releasing with a loud moan that made me wetter than I already was.

"Gotdamn, Aleesa," he huffed, sounding pissed off.

That was a good sign. Licking my lips, I boldly stood in front of the window, sure to give our audience a view of us naked. While he was sculpted like an African King, my body was stacked nicely too. Even if it wasn't, I was still showing it off and damn proud of it.

As I struggled to slide my costume back on, Rich helped me out. Gone were my stockings that he'd ripped to shreds, so I only had on my onesie.

"Put this on," he said, handing me his robe.

Sliding my arms into the sleeves, I tied the belt and thanked him. What I thought would be the walk of shame back into the house wasn't. Everyone had disappeared from the living room area. Pulling my phone from my wristlet, I went to call Kharisma, but she and Wayne walked back inside the house before I could.

"Hey!" She yelled out. "We're back. We had to drop off some folk that got too drunk."

"You like hearing yourself echo?" Rich asked with a chuckle. "You loud."

"Sorry. I just had to make my presence known louder this time," she said giving me a smirk. That let me know she and everyone else had possibly seen what we had been up to. "Leese, you ready?"

"Yeah."

Walking over to Rich, he licked those lips of his that I wish I had gotten a chance to feel all over my body and pulled me into him.

"You gone leave me in this big ass house by myself?"

Chuckling, I held him tighter. "Don't tell me

37

you're scared. You've been here all by yourself before now."

"You right. I'm just fucking with you. Call my phone, so I can have your number."

Not seeing a reason why he couldn't have my number, I handed my phone over to him. When his phone rang, he declined the call and handed it back to me. Pulling me into another hug, he kissed my cheek and let me go.

"A'ight, Aleesa. It was a pleasure."

I blushed. "Same. Hopefully, I'll see you around and not just in my daydreams."

"Hopefully."

Not wanting to prolong my stay or our parting words, Kharisma and I headed out the door and to her car that was parked right in front of the steps. On wobbly legs, I plopped myself into her passenger seat with a smile on my face.

"That good, huh?" Kharisma asked before she could even pull out of the driveway.

"Better than you think."

4

Aleesa

For as long as I had been paying rent, nothing irked my soul more than the first of the month rolling up on me like I stole something. That was the first thing on my mind when I woke up this morning. It was like every time I blinked, bills were due. Honestly, this adulting shit was for the birds. All ten thousand of their species, to be exact. Groaning, I rolled over in my bed. Last night seemed like a blur, but my aching limbs, swollen pussy, and the cash on my dresser was evidence that we'd had a damn good night.

Reaching for my phone, I rolled my eyes at a text from Coop and Kent. I bypassed whatever it was they were saying and opened the one from Rich. I'd texted him when we made it home last night and saved his number.

As sore as I was, his text had me sitting completely up in bed. "Is this a joke?" I asked aloud.

Rich: *It's the first of the month. You need your rent paid?*

"Lord, remember when I kept saying I see what you do for others? I just want to thank you right now in advance for all these blessings."

I had to give Him the praise first because, what? No man has ever in the history of my twenty-nine years of living offered to pay my rent. They might've said it jokingly, but no one had ever followed through. Before I could get my hopes up with Rich, I texted him back.

If you're offering, sure.

Rich: *What's the name of your complex or land-lord's info?*

Alpine Condos. Aleesa Donovan.

My thumbs moved quickly while replying just in case he wanted to change his mind. I waited for a good two minutes expecting a reply, but one never came. All he did was give the text a thumbs up. Not wanting to dwell on if he was really going to pay it or not, I climbed from the bed and headed to the bathroom.

After handling my hygiene, I peeked in on Kharisma, who was still knocked out and cuddled up with who I already knew was Wayne. Normally on mornings after drinking heavily, I'd have a hangover and not be in the mood for food. Today was totally different. My stomach was touching my back and growling like I hadn't eaten in days.

In the mood for some breakfast, but not in the mood to cook, I decided to run to a local deli about fifteen minutes away. They had the best fried pota- toes, and biscuits with gravy. Sliding on a hoodie, some leggings, and my UGG boots, I snatched up my wristlet from last night along with my keys and cell phone. On the drive over, I couldn't help but think about what all occurred last night.

I'd heard people talk about going on a bad trip off drugs but never thought I'd experience it one day. The crazy thing was, I hadn't done any drugs. The edible we took hadn't caused that much damage, I'm sure. Whatever Jennifer had given me, I had to know. Making a quick detour, I made my way to *Ace Liquors*.

Walking inside, I greeted the actual owner Aceshon, a thirty-something black businessman who all the women in our town had a crush on at one point in time. Too bad he was happily married and very much faithful with his fine ass.

"Hey, Ace," I waved. "Good morning."

"What's going on, Aleesa. You out early on a Sunday."

"Running to get some food. Is Jennifer in? She was bartending last night."

He tilted his head toward the back of the store. "Yep. She should be at the bar."

"Thank you."

Making my way toward the back of the store, another wave of déjà vu hit me. I stopped midstride and shook my head. This was crazy. Posted behind the bar taking inventory, Jennifer smiled when she saw me walking her way.

"You're back so soon. How was your night?"

"I'm not quite sure how to describe it yet, but I think I may still be feeling whatever it is you gave me. What was that shot?"

Wiping her hands on a dishrag, Jennifer came from around the bar and sat down in a highchair next to me. Facing me, she popped her hands open, making me jump a bit.

"The red or blue pill."

"What?"

"Choose one. If you pick red, I can reveal the truth about last night and what's to come. If you pick blue, you can remain on this blissful high and enjoy it for as long as it'll last."

I frowned. "But how long will it last?"

"For however long the other parties want it to."

"What other parties?"

She tipped her head to the side and grinned. "I think you know who. Whatever you wished for will only last as long as the person who fulfilled your wishes want them too."

"And that's if I pick the blue pill?"

"Mhm. If you pick the red, it all ends now regardless of the other parties, and you find out some harsh truths."

I gulped. I was not big on lies being revealed to me in an unpleasant manner. That derived from my biological dad telling me lies at a young age. I was one of those kids whose dad said they'd pick them up at this time on this day, but never showed. Our relationship was better now that I was grown, but I'd always remember my childhood traumas. Thank God for my stepdad.

With my mind made up, I reached for the blue pill. Satisfied with my answer, I sat back in my seat.

"So, what now? You never told me what was in that shot?"

"Eh. It was a potion that I was called to concoct for you. Don't ask me why. I just answer to my ancestors."

"I was hallucinating, and Rich could hear my thoughts."

"Whatever potion he was given allowed him to do that. Did I know it'd be him you'd meet? Absolutely not, but I see it worked out. Did the potion and he grant some of your wishes?"

Smiling, I nodded my head. "Yes. More than I could have imagined."

"Good. That's what I'm here for."

"Well, thank you. I feel like I should pay you for doing this for me."

Jennifer shook her head no. "Absolutely not. I'm rich in health and in wealth already. Spend that money on you some breakfast."

I gasped, and she grinned.

"I can only hear your thoughts when you're near me. But your stomach is growling too."

Laughing, I and thanked her again before heading out of the store.

Slightly baffled, I stayed in the parking lot for a good five minutes. I'd chosen the blue pill, but for how long would it choose me? And what all did that entail? This was a lot. I thought my mind was a fuzzy mess yesterday; I could only imagine what my days ahead would bring.

After picking up some breakfast for all three of us, I headed back to our condo. Kharisma and Wayne had just woken up from the sounds of it. Not wanting to hear them have morning sex, I slipped into my bedroom and closed the door. Finally, looking at my phone, I didn't see a text from Rich.

Okay. So, I was in my feelings a bit, but so what. He could've at least asked how my morning was or that he'd paid my rent. Wanting to see for myself if he was true to his word, I called the front office. I was so happy they were open seven days a week.

"Good morning. You've reached Alpine Condos. This is Kadi. How can I help you?"

"Hey, Kadi. It's Aleesa."

"Oh, hey girl! I was just about to send you an email."

That piqued my interest. "Really? About what?"

"Well, I just got off the phone with a very nice man who let us know your rent for the next year would be taken care of."

The phone slipped from my hand. Too stunned to cry, tears pooled in my eyes and settled as I tried to tell myself to breathe. Was this real life? Clearing my suddenly aching throat, I picked the phone back up.

"Ms. Aleesa? You still there?" Kadi asked.

"I-I'm. Y-Yes. I'm sorry. Could you repeat that for me?"

"Yes, of course. A guy called in and let us know he wanted to pay your rent up until November 1st of next year. Should we not have authorized this payment? I'm so sorry. We should've called you first."

"No, no. It's fine. I'm just in a bit of shock right now. So I can log onto my portal and there will be a credit on there?"

"That's correct. One of us will be by to drop off the statement sometime this week."

"Okay. Thank you. Have a good day."

She told me to do the same as I hurriedly logged into my resident portal. Nerves rattled; my hands shook as I tapped on the payment option. In bold green colored font was the largest dollar amount in credits I'd ever seen.

The tears fell then. I sobbed like a baby, because what... the... fuck. While I simply thought Rich would pay my rent for one month, he went above and fucking beyond for me. Rushing to our text messages, I sent him a bunch of crying faces because that's exactly what I was still doing. They were happy tears, of course. I texted him thank you in all caps, with a kissy face.

Rich: *I told you to be careful what you wish for.*

He absolutely had.

One Year Later

My first wish a year ago was for a man who willingly provided for me.

My second wish was for a man who could fulfill my sexual desires and fantasies.

Had I not chosen the blue pill, who knows how my life a year ago would have ended up. Rich had come into my life on Halloween night and literally spooked the fuck out of me.

He was all man, about his business, and about me.

He let that be known very clear. Whatever I wanted, he provided without protest. Trips out the country, startup money for my haircare line, random gifts with money included and so much more than I expected. With ease, he had spoiled me rotten and I loved it here. Well... I did until now.

I couldn't help but be extremely sad because what we shared was all ending today. Financially, I was set for a nice while, and was so sexually satisfied to the point where another nigga couldn't even enter my mind.

"You sure you're okay?" Kharisma asked, being her caring self like always.

I nodded my head, but deep down I was in my feelings and would be for a while. Thankfully, she didn't urge me to verbally tell her how I was feeling. Nostalgia swept over me like a hurricane wind as we pulled onto the street of what used to be Rich's home. The same home that I'd visited a year ago to date.

In the yard was a for sale sign.

Rich was leaving our city, and I had no clue as to where. See, the thing about the potion, the pill I chose, and my wishes was that they all worked on one accord. What I wished for I had been granted. It was much more than I expected and certainly less.

While I was trying to pursue a relationship with

Rich and make things official, he'd gently remind me that commitment isn't what I wished for. Having him all to myself besides financially and sexually wasn't his duty. He provided where it mattered most, and there was nothing I could do about it. Even if my emotions and heart had gotten involved.

I guess trickin' really is only a treat for as long as you let it be.

The End.

Special shout out to my fav, Wayne. Alongside Richmond aka Scritchmatic. One tweet from y'all urged me to change my character names and they fit perfectly.

Sequaia, Bianca, & Jah, thank y'all for putting up with me all day before this released. Lol! As always, y'all came through for me in the clutch. Love y'all!

To my readers,
I know this read was much different from what you're used to from me, but I hope you enjoyed it. I wanted to try my hand in a new genre and I loved it! Erotica seems to be my thing as well now, so we'll see where that goes.
If you loved Rich and Aleesa's story, be sure to drop me a review on any social media platforms. Since this wasn't released on AMZN yet, I don't have a place for

reviews to go. I would truly appreciate it. Tell a friend about this book and remember… be careful what you wish for.

Facebook: https://www.facebook.com/briann.danae

Instagram: https://www.instagram.com/brianndanae/

Made in the USA
Las Vegas, NV
15 February 2025